DESIGNED BY RUTH HELLER

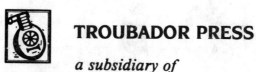

TROUBADOR PRESS

a subsidiary of

PRICE STERN SLOAN

Los Angeles

Work through the maze numerically,
ending at number six.

20 19 18 17 16 15 14 13 12

SOLUTION TO MAZE 1

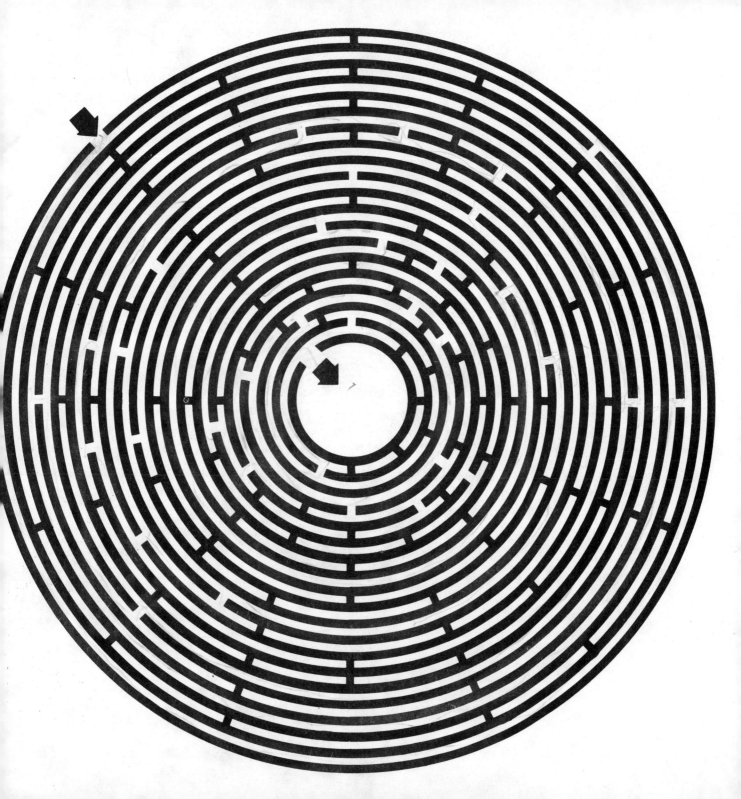

Weave over and under, but *do not cross a line,*
to connect each one of the three symbols to its mate.

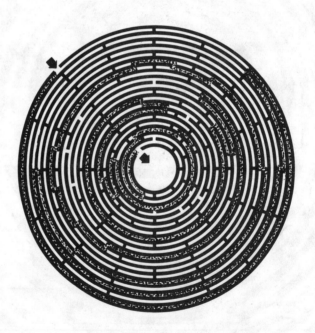

SOLUTION TO MAZE 2

SOLUTION TO MAZE 3

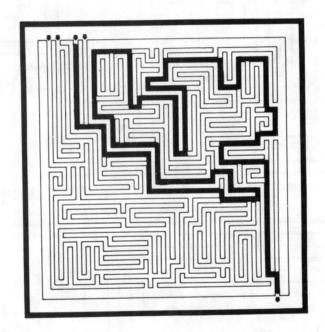

SOLUTION TO MAZE 4

Find the paths connecting the *mismatched* symbols, black to white.
Weave under and over, but do not cross a line.

SOLUTION TO MAZE 5

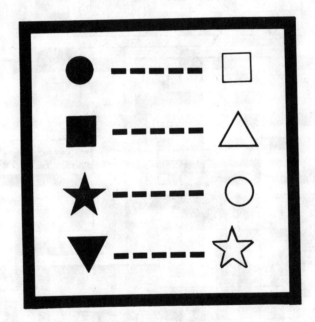

SOLUTION TO MAZE 6

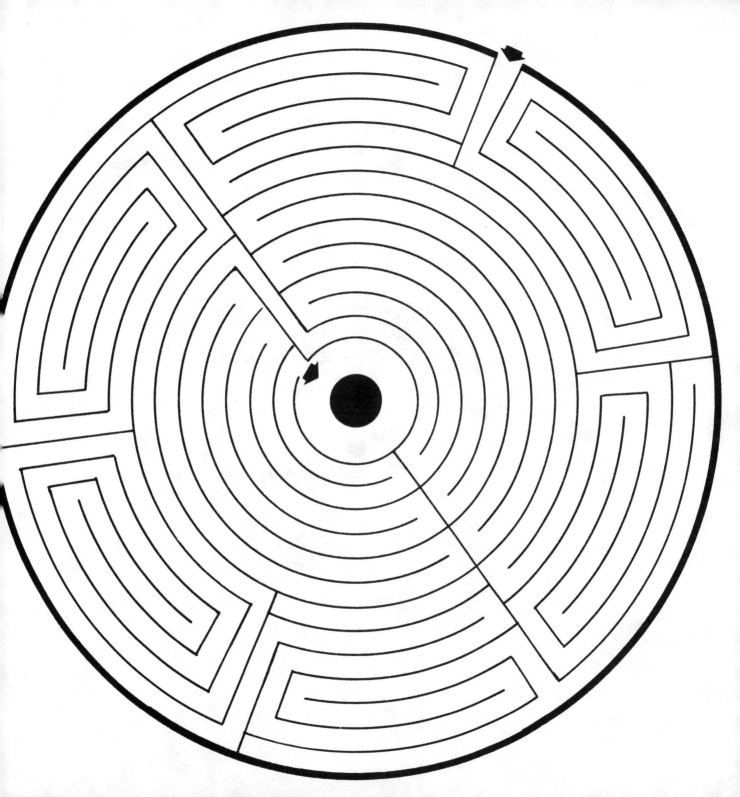

SOLUTION TO MAZE 7

ENTER

EXIT

This maze is completed only by winding through all four outposts.

9

SOLUTION TO MAZE 8

Exit

SOLUTION TO MAZE 9

SOLUTION TO MAZE 10

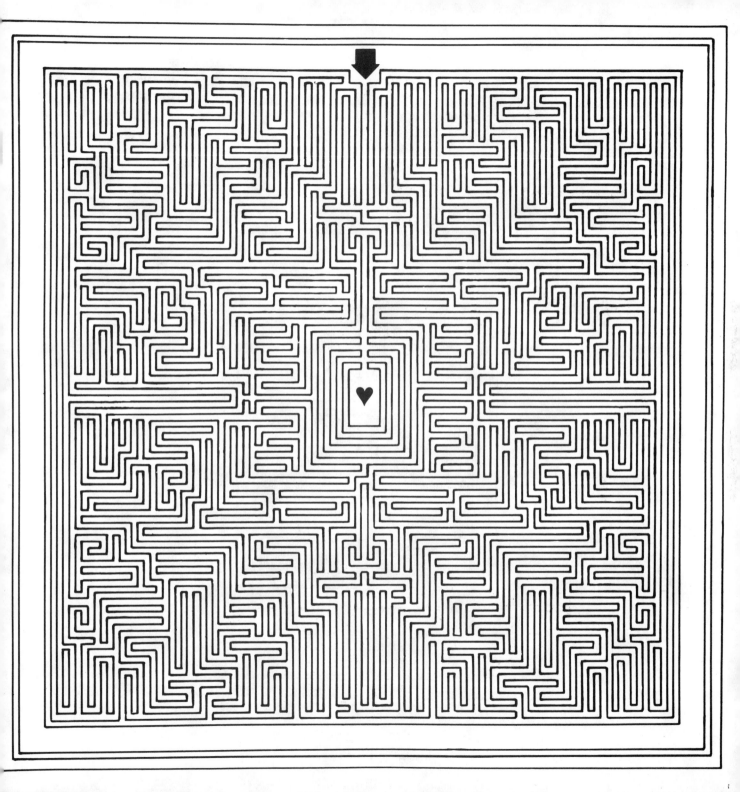

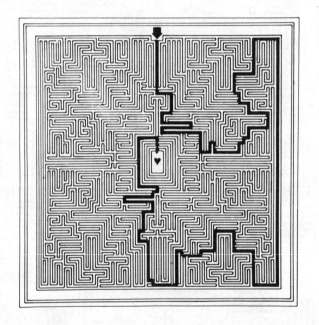

SOLUTION TO MAZE 11

SOLUTION TO MAZE 12

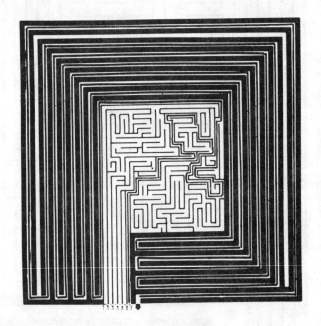

SOLUTION TO MAZE 13

SOLUTION TO MAZE 14

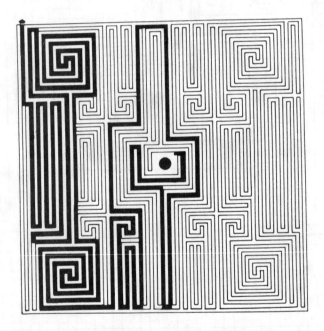

SOLUTION TO MAZE 15

SOLUTION TO MAZE 16

SOLUTION TO MAZE 17

CLOSED LANE

OPEN LANE

SOLUTION TO MAZE 18

More exciting, mind-bending challenges can be found in:

HIDDEN PICTURE COLORING BOOKS:
Cars, Trucks, Trains & Planes
Cities
Creatures of the Deep
Fairy Tales
Farm
Pets
Playground
School
Toys
Under the Big Top
Weird & Wacky Animals
Zoo

The above books, and many others, may be bought wherever books are sold,
or may be ordered directly from the publisher.

PRICE STERN SLOAN
Los Angeles